A Note to Parents and Caregivers:

With a focus on math, science, and social studies, *Read-it!* Readers support both the learning of content information and the extension of more complex reading skills. They encourage the development of problem-solving skills that help children expand their thinking.

The PURPLE LEVEL presents basic topics and objects using high frequency words and simple language patterns.

The RED LEVEL presents familiar topics using common words and repeating sentence patterns.

The BLUE LEVEL presents new ideas using a larger vocabulary and varied sentence structure.

The YELLOW LEVEL presents more challenging ideas, a broad vocabulary, and wide variety in sentence structure.

The GREEN LEVEL presents more complex ideas, an extended vocabulary range, and expanded language structures.

The ORANGE LEVEL presents a wide range of ideas and concepts using challenging vocabulary and complex language structures.

When sharing a content focused book with your child, read to find out facts and concepts, pausing often to restate and talk about the new information. The realistic story format provides an opportunity to talk about the language used, and to learn about reading to problem-solve for information. Encourage children to measure, make maps, and consider other situations that allow them to apply what they are learning.

There is no right or wrong way to share books with children. Find time to read and share new learning with your child, and pass on the legacy of literacy.

Adria F. Klein, Ph.D.
Professor Emeritus
California State University
San Bernardino, California

Editor: Christianne Jones
Designer: Amy Muehlenhardt
Page Production: Ashlee Schultz
Art Director: Nathan Gassman
The illustrations in this book were created digitally.

Picture Window Books
5115 Excelsior Boulevard
Suite 232
Minneapolis, MN 55416
877-845-8392
www.picturewindowbooks.com

Library of Congress Cataloging-in-Publication Data
Aboff, Marcie.
Shells alive / by Marcie Aboff ; illustrated by Amy Bailey Muehlenhardt.
p. cm. — (Read-it! readers: math)
ISBN-13: 978-1-4048-4210-6 (library binding)
[1. Addition—Fiction.] I. Muehlenhardt, Amy Bailey, 1974- ill. II. Title.
PZ7.A164She 2008
[E]—dc22   2007032903

Shells Alive

by Marcie Aboff
illustrated by Amy Bailey Muehlenhardt

Special thanks to our advisers for their expertise:

Stuart Farm, M.Ed.
Mathematics Lecturer, University of North Dakota
Grand Forks, North Dakota

Adria F. Klein, Ph.D.
Professor Emeritus, California State University
San Bernardino, California

PiCTURE WiNDOW BOOKS
Minneapolis, Minnesota

Kim and Josh were going to stay at their Grandma's beach house for a week. They couldn't wait to get there.

"At Grandma's house, I'm going to the beach every day!" Kim told her parents.
"Me, too!" her brother said.

"Hello everyone!" Grandma said.
"Where are your bathing suits? I'm ready
to hit the beach!"

Kim and Josh ran upstairs and changed. They were in such a rush that they almost forgot to say goodbye to their parents.

Kim, Josh, and Grandma grabbed towels, sunblock, and sand pails, and they walked to the beach.

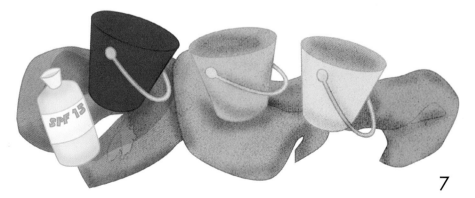

Grandma found a clear spot close to the ocean. Kim dropped her towel and sand pails. She ran toward the ocean and splashed into the cool waves. Grandma and Josh followed right behind her.

After a long swim and lunch, Kim and Josh became tired and bored.

"What can we do now?" they asked.

"Let's collect seashells. That's my favorite hobby," Grandma said.

They took their pails and walked along the beach.

"Look at this pretty seashell," Kim said.
"That's a scallop shell," Grandma said.
"Do you see all of the colors on it?"

"This shell is so cool," said Josh.
"What is it called?"

   "That's a moon shell," said Grandma.
"A snail used to live in that shell."

Kim and Josh collected all kinds of shells.
"How many shells do you have, Josh?"
Grandma asked.

"I have nineteen," he said.

"And I have eighteen," Kim said.

"You have thirty-seven shells altogether," Grandma said.

Nineteen plus eighteen equals thirty-seven.

19 + 18 = 37

Kim, Josh, and Grandma walked over to the dock. There were even more shells there. Kim collected seventeen more shells.

Kim added seventeen shells to her eighteen for a sum of thirty-five.

$$17 + 18 = 35$$

Josh collected nineteen more shells.

Josh added nineteen shells to his nineteen for a sum of thirty-eight.

$$19 + 19 = 38$$

"Wow, that's seventy-three shells. That's a lot of shells for one day of collecting," said Grandma.

Thirty-five plus thirty-eight equals seventy-three.

$$35 + 38 = 73$$

The next day, they went to the beach again. Kim and Josh didn't want to swim or build a castle. They wanted to collect more shells.

Josh collected eighteen more shells. He couldn't wait to add those to the thirty-eight he had found yesterday.

Josh added eighteen shells to his thirty-eight for a sum of fifty-six.

18 + 38 = 56

Kim began looking for more shells, too. She
bent down to pick one up, but the shell moved!
It moved all by itself!

Kim called to Grandma. She pointed to the moving shell.

"Look!" she exclaimed. "That shell is alive! It's moving by itself!"

"That's a hermit crab," Grandma said with a laugh. "The shell is the crab's home. Usually hermit crabs travel in packs. I'll bet there are more hermit crabs around here."

Grandma was right. Kim and Josh saw lots of moving shells.

"Wow! They're so cool," said Josh.
Kim and Josh watched the crabs for a
long time.

The next night, Kim, Josh, and Grandma
walked along the boardwalk.

They went on rides. They played games.

Then they passed a pet store on the boardwalk. There were two big tanks of hermit crabs in the store window.

"Look! They're selling hermit crabs," said Kim.

"Can I hold one?" Kim asked the sales clerk. "Sure," he said. "Put your palm out, and I'll grab one for you."

"I wish I had a hermit crab," said Kim.
"Me, too," said Josh.

They both looked up at Grandma.
"You'll have to ask your mom and
dad," she said.

That night Kim and Josh called their parents.

"They said yes!" Kim said. "We have to promise to take care of them."

The next day, they went back to the store. Kim and Josh each picked out one hermit crab. The sales clerk told them how to take care of their new pets. They bought a tank, food, sand, and climbing toys.

On Saturday, their parents picked them up.
Buckets of shells waited on the front porch.

"Look at all those seashells!" said their mom.

"I collected thirty-five seashells," said Kim

"And I collected fifty-six," said Josh.

"That's ninety-one shells to take home!" said their dad.

Kim added her thirty-five shells to Josh's fifty-six for a sum of ninety-one.

$$35 + 56 = 91$$

"We have two more shells to show you.
Except they're not just shells," Kim said.
"Meet my hermit crab. His name is Scallop."
"And mine is Moon," said Josh.
"These are our favorite shells of all!"
Kim said. "What a great vacation!"

Addition Activity

What you need:
- 16 small pieces of paper
- pen or pencil
- at least two people

What you do:
1. Write down eight double-digit addition problems that use regrouping. You can use examples from this book.
2. Write the problem on one piece of paper, and the answer on another.
3. Turn the pieces of paper over.
4. Mix them up and put them in four rows of four.
5. Take turns turning over two pieces of paper. If you match the problem to the answer, take another turn. If you don't, it's the next player's turn.
6. Keep playing until all of the pairs are matched up.
7. The player with the most pairs wins.

Glossary

add—to find the sum of two or more numbers
collect—to gather
equal—being the same in amount
sum—the number you get when you add two or more numbers together

To Learn More

More Books to Read

Murphy, Stuart J. *Mall Mania.* New York: HarperCollins, 2006.
Slater, Teddy, and Marilyn Burns. *98, 99, 100, Ready or Not, Here I come!* New York: Scholastic, 1999.
Wright, Alexandra. *Alice in Pastaland: A Math Adventure.* Watertown, Mass.: Charlesbridge, 1997.

On the Web

FactHound offers a safe, fun way to find Web sites related to topics in this book. All of the sites on FactHound have been researched by our staff.

1. Visit *www.facthound.com*
2. Type in this special code: 1404842101
3. Click on the FETCH IT button.

Your trusty FactHound will fetch the best sites for you!

Look for all of the books in the
Read-it! Readers: Math series:

The Guessing Game (math: weight)
The Lemonade Standoff (math: two-digit addition without regrouping)
Mike's Mystery (math: two-digit subtraction without regrouping)
The Pizza Palace (math: fractions)
The Pool Party (math: temperature)
Shells Alive (two-digit addition with regrouping)
The Tallest Snowman (math: measurements)
Too Many Tomatoes (math: two-digit subtraction with regrouping)